Miss Spider's New Car

paintings and verse by David Kirk

PUFFIN

A CALLAWAY EDITION

"MUM writes that we should come to tea.
Let's go!" Miss Spider cried.
"We'll hire a frog to cross the bog
Down to the riverside.
Among the mice, we might entice
A fuzzy woodland guide."

"Those mice could bite you!" Holley howled.
"The river's full of snakes.
To think of you atop a frog
Gives me the quiver-shakes.
It's much too far. Let's buy a car
Instead, for heaven's sakes!"

"You're brilliant, dear!" Miss Spider cheered.
"A car would be divine.
With sky-blue shells and silver bells
And chiming bits that shine.
Look over there! I do declare
That one would suit us fine!"

BUB BUMBLE'S BUGGIES

Miss Spider grinned, "We'll take it home!"
But Holley only frowned.
"Would it be wise to buy the first
Jalopy that we've found?
I'll ask the bee to wait 'til three
So we can shop around."

Mik Mantis crooned, "This honey runs
On nectar from a flower.
Its two-stem engine is equipped
With turbo-bumble power,
And capable of reaching speeds
Near ninety yards per hour!"

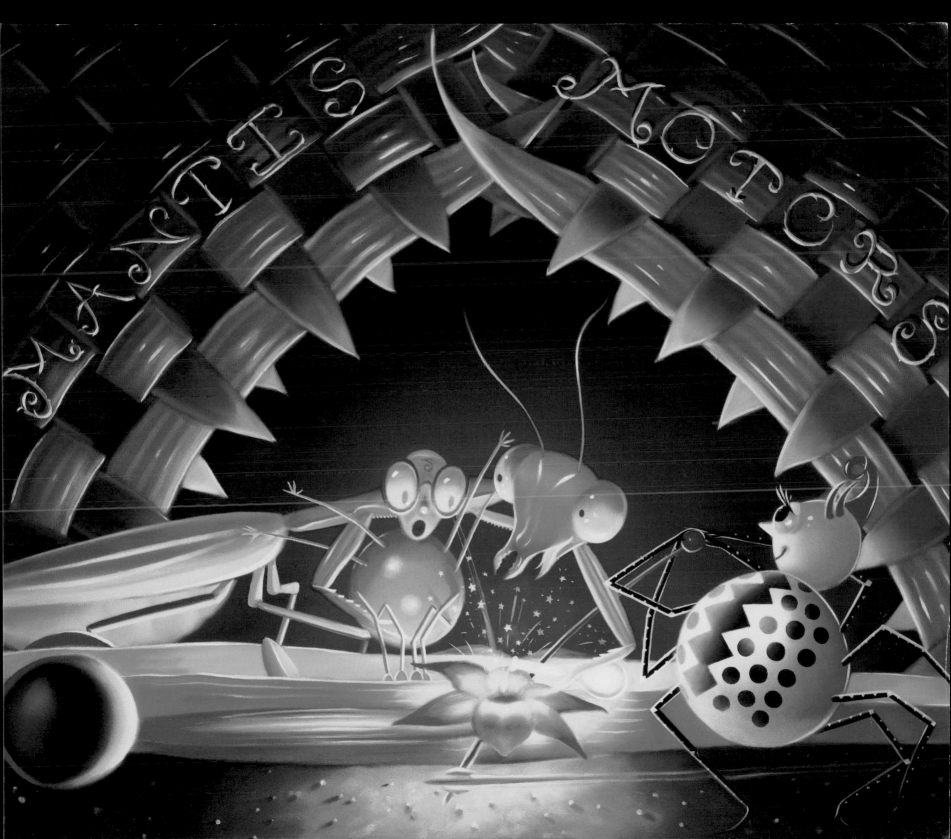

DEEP HOLE !

Poor Holley shrieked, "It's much too fast!
Please look out where you're going.
There might be hungry rats down there.
We have no way of knowing."
"How fine it is," Miss Spider laughed,
"To feel my toppy blowing!"

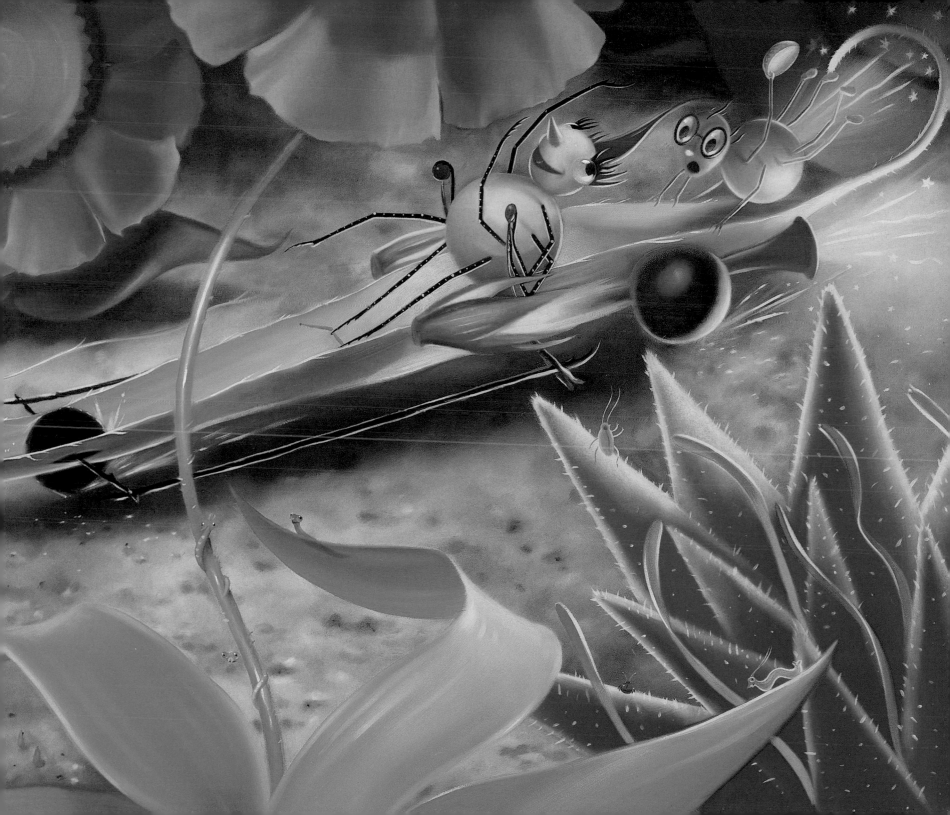

"Slick-tail the snail," said Holley,
"Calls this gem the Escargot.
It looks all sleek and spirally,
But rides so nice and slow."
"That sales snail," said Miss Spider,
"Looks familiar, don't you know?"

"The wheel is out of date," whooped Hop,
"Just like a dinosaur.
Our flexo-flea spring-loaded legs
Are what you're looking for.
Just pull the round brown throttle down
And hear that engine roar!"

"Why travel on the public roads?
Such trouble that it brings:
The bumps and holes, the toads and moles,
The snakes and rats and things.
It's only sense," Meg Mayfly bragged,
"To buy this car with wings!"

Meg's
Wings
n'
Things

"It's almost three now," Holley coughed.
"We really ought to run.
I'm certain, dear, the first car was
By far the nicest one."
"Just try this dream," Sid Skipper schemed,
"And then you shall be done."

"The springs are shot," Miss Spider moaned.
"I bounce with every bump.
The steering's locked. The brakes won't work,
No matter how I pump.
That tree is getting awfully close –
I think we'd better jump!"

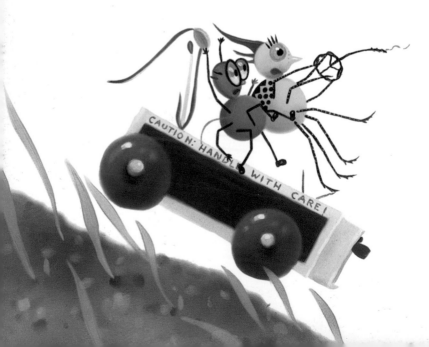

Miss Spider wailed, "They'll sell my car.
It's nearly half past three!"
Then Holley spied a dozing moth
And whispered secretly,
"Excuse me, Sue, but could you do
A courtesy for me?"

"Oh, where's my car? My lovely car!"
She blew her nose and cried.
"A moth paid cash and drove it home,"
Bub Bumble Bee replied.
"I'm sorry, ma'am. Indeed I am."
"Me too," Miss Spider sighed.

But then upon Miss Spider's lawn . . .
Oh, what a dazzling sight!
Proud Holley beamed, "Moth Sue came through,
The way I hoped she might.
You knew it from the first, my love,
That little car's just right!"

Beneath the door, upon the floor,
Miss Spider found a note.
"Another message from my mum,
I wonder what she wrote . . .

"What fun! She wants to take us both
Out shopping for a boat!"